# BAKUGAN
## BATTLE BRAWLERS

# DARKUS RISING

BY TRACEY WEST

SCHOLASTIC INC.

NEW YORK    TORONTO    LONDON    AUCKLAND

SYDNEY    MEXICO CITY    NEW DELHI    HONG KONG

NO PART OF THIS PUBLICATION MAY BE REPRODUCED IN WHOLE OR IN PART, OR STORED IN A RETRIEVAL SYSTEM, OR TRANSMITTED IN ANY FORM OR BY ANY MEANS, ELECTRONIC, MECHANICAL, PHOTOCOPYING, RECORDING, OR OTHERWISE, WITHOUT WRITTEN PERMISSION OF THE PUBLISHER. FOR INFORMATION REGARDING PERMISSION, WRITE TO SCHOLASTIC INC., ATTENTION: PERMISSIONS DEPARTMENT, 557 BROADWAY, NEW YORK, NY 10012.

ISBN-13: 978-0-545-15521-2
ISBN-10: 0-545-15521-5

© SPIN MASTER LTD/SEGA TOYS.

BAKUGAN AND BATTLE BRAWLERS, AND ALL RELATED TITLES, LOGOS, AND CHARACTERS ARE TRADEMARKS OF SPIN MASTER LTD. NELVANA IS A TRADEMARK OF NELVANA LIMITED. CORUS IS A TRADEMARK OF CORUS ENTERTAINMENT INC. USED UNDER LICENSE BY SCHOLASTIC INC. ALL RIGHTS RESERVED.

PUBLISHED BY SCHOLASTIC INC. SCHOLASTIC AND ASSOCIATED LOGOS ARE TRADEMARKS AND/OR REGISTERED TRADEMARKS OF SCHOLASTIC INC.

12 11 10 9 8 7 6 5 4 3 2          9 10 11 12 13 14/0

COVER ART BY CARLO LORASO
PRINTED IN THE U.S.A.
FIRST PRINTING, AUGUST 2009

# THE STORY SO FAR

**D**an Kuso and his friends have been busy. The masked brawler, Masquerade, has been sending brawlers to challenge them in battle. Masquerade's brawlers come armed with the Doom Card, which gives them the power to send losing Bakugan to the terrible Doom Dimension.

When they're not brawling, Dan and his friends have been trying to figure out what's happening in Vestroia. This parallel world is the home to all Bakugan. They know that a Bakugan named Naga tried to absorb all of the power in Vestroia. But he failed. Though he managed to steal the Infinity Core, he lost the Silent Core. Their mission is to find the two cores and defeat Naga — or both the human world and Vestroia will fall.

Dan tried to recruit top-ranked brawler, Shun, to join him and his friends in their fight. At first, Shun didn't want anything to do with it. But once he realized that Masquerade was up to no good, Shun decided to help.

Now it's up to Dan, Runo, Marucho, Julie, Shun, and Alice to save the day. But Masquerade has a new plan to stop them. . . .

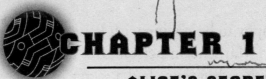

# CHAPTER 1

## ALICE'S SECRET

**M**oonlight shone into Runo's bedroom window. The whole room glowed with soft blue light.

Runo was lying under the covers, talking a mile a minute. Her friend Alice from Moscow was tucked into a cot on the floor.

"Yeah, my dad's totally stoked that you decided to stay with us," Runo said. "He said, 'we're gonna get a lot more customers with you working for us!' "

Runo's parents owned a restaurant. Runo helped out by waiting tables there. Red-haired Alice was pretty and sweet, and the customers really liked her.

"I won't be the star attraction anymore," Runo said cheerfully. "You'll get all the attention now!"

Alice didn't answer. She gazed up at the ceiling, her brown eyes full of worry.

She was happy to be staying with Runo. It was nice to meet Dan and Marucho in person after talking to them all on the Internet. But Alice had a secret — a secret she was afraid to share.

Her mind drifted back to a meeting with the brawlers not long ago. They had figured out that a human scientist, Michael, had somehow traveled to Vestroia and was helping Naga. Dan was really angry. He wanted to find Michael and stop him, fast.

Alice was in shock when she heard the news. Michael was her grandfather. He had gone missing months ago. Alice had no idea he had ended up in Vestroia.

*I haven't told anyone about my grandfather Michael yet*, Alice thought. *Maybe it's time.*

She looked up at Runo. "Hey, Runo. You awake?"

But Runo was softly snoring.

Alice sighed and leaned back on her pillow. She didn't like keeping secrets from her friends. In the morning, she would tell them everything.

# CHAPTER 2

## A ROYAL BATTLE!

On the other side of the world, a white limo pulled up in front of a sprawling mansion. A Bakugan brawler named Billy stepped out of the car. Billy wore an orange and white baseball jacket and matching cap. His Subterra Cycloid was perched on his shoulder.

"I must be doing something right," Billy said, admiring the mansion. "I never thought I'd get invited to a place like this."

"It's 'cause you got talent, boss!" Cycloid told him. "You climbed to tenth place in the rankings in just a few days."

"Yeah, you're right. I deserve this," Billy said. His blue eyes shone with anticipation.

He walked up to the large front doors. They swung open before he could knock. Then he stepped into a large foyer. Marble columns rose up to meet the high ceiling. A long staircase covered in a red carpet led to the next floor.

Three brawlers in the room nodded to Billy. One was a giant teen with a bald head. The other was a girl with dark purple hair and serious eyes. The third was a young boy with a backward baseball cap on his curly dark hair. He was crouched on top of one of the columns.

Before Billy could introduce himself, another brawler stepped in the door behind him.

"I'm looking for the party for the top ten international Bakugan players. Is this the place?" he asked. He was tall, with silvery white hair and green eyes. He wore a formal-looking long, white coat over white pants tucked into riding boots. A ruffled scarf was tucked into his purple collar.

"Yeah," Billy replied.

"That's good!" the brawler said. "My ranking is number two. I'm Klaus."

"I'm Chan," called out the girl. She wore a striking red Chinese-style sleeveless jacket over red satin pants. "My ranking is third place!"

"My name's Julio," said the bald muscle teen. "I'm in fourth place!"

The boy in the backward cap jumped off of the column, somersaulting in midair. He landed gracefully on his feet.

"And I'm Komba," he announced. "My ranking is fifth place."

"Nice to meet you, I'm Billy," Billy said. "I've got the tenth place spot. Yeah!"

"Ha! Double digits!" Komba cried.

Billy didn't know what to say. He wasn't expecting any trash talking today.

"Which means that the first and sixth-to-ninth ranked battlers aren't here yet," Komba reasoned. "I guess they're running late."

"So what's up?" Julio asked. "When does this so-called party get started anyway?"

"Yeah, I don't see any decorations," Chan said suspiciously.

Komba held up an invitation. "You're right, but according to the map on this card, we're in the right place."

"Listen, it's not every day that the world's top-ranked Bakugan players are in the same room together," Klaus said eagerly. "Would any of you be interested in a little game?"

"I'm up for that!" Chan said quickly.

"Count me in," Julio added. "I know you all would think I didn't have the skills if I tried to back out on you."

"Yeah, I'm up for a battle," Komba said. "That sounds like fun to me!"

Klaus eyed Billy curiously. "And you?"

"I'm in! Let's do it!" Billy replied. So what if everyone ranked higher than he did? "Yeah!"

The five brawlers stood in a circle in the large room. Each one held up a Bakugan Gate Card.

"Bakugan! Field Open!" they all cried at once.

Symbols of the six worlds of Vestroia glowed on the cards, then emerged, swirling together in the center of the brawlers. Time in the human world came to a stop as the Bakugan field formed. The space between the brawlers was now blank and gray. Swirls of bright light made a shimmering wall all around them.

"If all five of us are in agreement, for the record this will be an Exhibition Battle," Klaus said. Then he quickly changed his mind. "No, wait. Speed Play!"

"What is a Speed Play?" Julio asked.

"Let's make it a Bakugan Royal Battle, since we're all in this together," Billy suggested.

Chan nodded. "Sure, I'll go along with that."

"I'm into it. Let's get started," Komba agreed.

In a normal battle, each player would throw out a Gate Card to start. In this Royal Battle, only one Gate Card would be thrown down. Then each player would throw down a Bakugan, one at a time. The strongest Bakugan left standing would be the winner.

"All right, the game is on!" Billy shouted. "Go, Cycloid!"

"Let me at 'em, boss!" Cycloid cheered.

Billy wound up his arm like a baseball pitcher and tossed Cycloid's brown Bakugan ball onto the field.

"Bakugan Brawl!" Billy shouted. "Cycloid Stand!"

The ball popped open, and Cycloid transformed into his true form. The big, brown monster had orange markings painted on his muscled chest. Cycloid had one giant eye in the center of his large head, and a short white horn right over the eye. He held a heavy club in his right hand.

Then Billy held up an Ability Card.

"Ability Card activate!" he called out. "Right Gigante!"

Cycloid's right arm grew in size. The Bakugan pounded his weapon on the Gate Card.

"Just try coming at me!" he challenged. "I'll make you a member of my special club!"

Komba wasn't impressed. "Ha! What a loudmouth," he said. He jumped in the air. "Bakugan Brawl!"

He tossed a green Bakugan ball onto the Gate Card with Cycloid.

"Harpus Stand!"

Light blazed as the Bakugan took on its true form. Ventus Harpus had the body of a woman, but talons and wings like a bird. Long, green tail feathers sprouted from her lower back. Her face wasn't quite human; her eyes were big and dark, she had sharp fangs in her mouth, and a head of wild green hair.

"Ventus Harpus! Ability Card Activate!" Komba cried. "Feather Blast!"

Harpus flapped her wings, and a great wind blew across the field. Cyclops roared as the wind nearly knocked the club out of his hand.

"Ha!" Komba said. Then he heard Chan call out behind him.

"Ability Activate! Face of Rage!"

Chan had thrown a Bakugan onto the field — Pyrus Fortress. The tall Bakugan looked like some mythical creature with four arms and four faces. Gold bands circled Fortress's arms and wrists.

When Chan used the Ability Card, Fortress held two

hands in front of his face. When he lifted them, his calm face was replaced by an angry one, with glowing green eyes and sharp teeth.

"You won't be able to beat Fortress's combined talents, beauty and strength!" Chan said proudly.

But before Fortress could make a move, a blinding light struck the field. The light came from a strange Bakugan that looked like a giant eyeball with tentacles extending all around it. Cycloid, Harpus, and Fortress tried to escape the bright light, but they all seemed to be frozen to the spot.

"Yeah!" Julio cheered. "Haos Tentaclear's eye has got you! You can't move!"

Klaus began to chuckle loudly. Julio turned to him, confused.

"Perfect!" Klaus said. "I didn't expect a battle with the top-ranked players would be this much fun."

"You sound confident, Klaus," Chan said.

Julio was annoyed. "Where's your Bakugan? Shoot it and get in the game!"

"Well, it's already in the battle," Klaus said coolly.

His four opponents frowned. "Huh?"

Klaus held up a card. "Ability Card Activate. Okay . . . use your singing voice on them!"

The center of the field began to shimmer. A strange, unearthly sound came from the same place. It echoed among the Bakugan like an eerie bell chiming.

The four Bakugan found themselves being drawn into the field's center. They couldn't stop.

A Bakugan in a turquoise dress rose up in the middle of them, carrying a golden harp. Her blue hair flowed down her back like an ocean wave. Her face had no nose or mouth, just two golden eyes.

"Allow me to introduce my beloved Aquos Sirenoid!" Klaus said.

Sirenoid clearly had more power than the other Bakugan. It looked like Klaus would win the Royal Battle.

*Crrrrrrrack!*

Jagged purple lightning suddenly streaked across the field. The brawlers shielded their eyes from the flashing purple light. Then a shadow appeared above them, slowly floating down toward them.

"Who's there?" Klaus called out.

The brawler was closer now. He wore a white suit and a light blue mask that covered his eyes and most of his face.

"My name is Masquerade."

# CHAPTER 3

## MASQUERADE'S PROPOSAL

Chan recognized the name. "You're the number-one-ranked player!"

Masquerade floated above them. "So you've heard of me before?"

"What do you want?" Klaus asked. "Have you come to join the battle?"

Masquerade chuckled. "No, but look at your feet."

The five brawlers looked down. The Bakugan field had disappeared. They were all floating in waves of eerie red light. In the center of them all was a large bubble with the shadow of a Dragonoid Bakugan inside it.

"What is this?" Klaus asked.

"The floor has disappeared?" Billy couldn't believe it.

"Is this some kind of trick?" Chan asked.

Komba frowned. "Where are we?"

"Hey, take us back to our world right now!" Julio demanded angrily.

"I'll take you back soon enough," Masquerade said.

From inside the bubble, the Dragonoid let out a roar.

"Humans!"

The startled brawlers gasped. The Bakugan's eyes glowed with purple light.

"Kneel before me, your new master!"

Then the bubble and red swirling light suddenly disappeared. They were all back in the foyer of the mansion. Masquerade stood on top of the red-carpeted staircase.

"I brought you all here today for an important reason," Masquerade announced. "I want you to get rid of Dan Kuso and the Bakugan Battle Brawlers. That will be your mission."

Klaus smiled. "Ha! Easy!"

"It will be an honor to take him down," Chan said.

Komba shook his fist. "Oh yeah. You want him out? No problem!"

"Come on. When do we start?" Julio asked eagerly.

Billy's eyes shone with confidence. "He's history! He doesn't have a chance!"

Cycloid joined in from on top of Billy's shoulder. "You said it, boss!"

Masquerade grinned. With the world's best brawlers on his side, Dan and his friends would soon be out of the way.

His master, Naga, would be so pleased!

# CHAPTER 4

## ALICE CONFESSES

Alice woke up late the next morning. She looked for Runo, but couldn't find her.

"She's at the store," Runo's mother told her. "I just sent her out to get a couple of things."

Alice went back to Runo's room, disappointed. "I finally get the courage to tell Runo about my grand-father and she's not even here."

She thought about telling Dan, but he had such a hot temper — he might get upset. There had to be someone else she could confide in. . . .

Alice smiled. She quickly got dressed in a sleeveless blue shirt, white shorts, and long yellow vest. Then she headed across town to Marucho's house.

Marucho's home was actually a towering skyscraper. When Alice arrived he led her up to his room, through the family art gallery and zoo, complete with giraffes, pandas, and elephants.

"What an honor," Marucho said. He was the youngest brawler, with a mop of yellow hair, bright blue eyes, and glasses. He always dressed in a white and blue sailor suit. "This is quite extraordinary, you coming to visit me all by yourself. I hope your visit has been satisfactory so far."

"Well, I . . . Marucho, I have something really important to tell you," Alice began.

"Really?" Marucho asked. His heart started to beat quickly.

"A confession," Alice said nervously. "Something I need you to hear me say."

Marucho's imagination took over. Alice looked so pretty, with her big, brown eyes. Had she come to confess something?

*Marucho, it's you* . . . he imagined her saying. *I always thought you were* . . .

But Alice was really saying, "My grandfather Michael."

"You always thought I was your grandfather Michael?" Marucho asked. Then he blushed, realizing how silly he sounded. "Alice, what did you say?"

"You know that missing scientist Michael Gehahbich? Well, he's my grandfather," Alice told him.

Marucho was shocked. "WHAAAAAT?"

Marucho's voice echoed throughout the mansion. But he quickly got over his surprise. Soon, Runo had finished her errands and joined them, along with Dan. They gathered in Marucho's room, where he contacted Julie and Shun on his computer. The two brawlers' faces looked down on them from a giant video screen. Alice sat in the big green office chair behind Marucho's desk. Three Bakugan sat on the desktop: Dan's Drago, Marucho's Preyas, and Runo's Tigrerra.

"Really? Michael is your grandfather?" Dan asked.

"Yes," Alice said. "That day when the Bakugan and all the cards appeared, that was the day my grandfather disappeared. I didn't see him again until about six months later."

Alice remembered that day well. She had been studying her Bakugan cards when Grandfather Michael had appeared in the doorway. She ran into his arms, thrilled. But Michael had frowned when he saw the Bakugan card in her hand.

"He seemed very surprised," Alice explained. "But the strange thing is, that day when Dan met Drago, my grandfather disappeared again. I haven't heard a thing from him since."

"You kept that a secret from us?" Dan asked. "Thanks for telling us, Alice. Oh man, that must have been hard."

Alice sighed with relief. "Oh, I'm sorry! I thought you would overreact. I had you all wrong."

Runo turned to Dan and grinned. "You overreact?" she asked in mock disbelief.

Up on the video screen, Julie scowled. "Runo and Alice! I think you're just trying to get Dan's attention."

"Why would we want to do that?" Runo asked. "That's so lame!"

Drago was more interested in what Alice had to say.

"Have you heard anything about the collapse of Vestroia?" he asked her.

"Nothing, Drago," Alice replied. "But if all the stories we've been hearing are true and my grandfather really did go to Vestroia, we may find something in his laboratory. Unfortunately, it's in Moscow."

"I guess we'll have to go to his laboratory then!" Dan said.

Runo rolled her eyes. "Sure, let's go. But didn't you

listen to Alice's story? Her grandfather's lab is in Moscow!"

"It's important that we go there," Shun urged.

"Yeah, sure, that's great," Runo said. "Just how are we gonna do that?"

Marucho grinned. "Leave it to me. I know a way!"

# CHAPTER 5
## MICHAEL'S STORY

The next morning, Marucho's butler, Kato, drove a black limo up to Dan's house. Dan ran out of the building, a backpack on his back. His mom and dad stood at the door to watch him go.

"Bye, I'm off to Moscow!" Dan called out cheerfully.

Kato emerged from the car. He was tall and thin. A ring of fluffy white hair circled his bald head. He had a mustache to match. As always, he wore a neat black suit.

"Ma'am, please don't worry. I assure you I will take good care of your son," he said.

Dan's mom gave him a grateful smile. "Yes, please take care of our boy. He can be quite a handful!"

Kato picked up Runo and Alice. He took them all to an underground airplane hangar. Marucho's family plane had four large engines, two over each wing, that looked like they belonged on a rocket ship. The inside cabin looked like a comfortable living room, with purple couches and a large TV screen.

Dan, Runo, Alice, and Marucho took their seats. Kato started the engines, and the plane began to rumble. It rose up on a mechanical platform that pushed the plane up through the underground hangar and right through a lake up above! Dan gazed out of the window in amazement as the waters parted and the plane launched into the air.

"Oh wow. Awesome!" Dan cried.

Runo looked pale. "Oh, my stomach. I'll lose my lunch!"

The plane zoomed forward. They quickly sped over the city. Then Kato's voice came over the radio.

"Sir, I'm going to fly over Master Shun's dojo now," he reported.

Shun's family dojo was a small compound of sprawling buildings in the middle of the woods. Shun stood on the roof. As the plane approached, he calmly threw a rope over the wing and then climbed aboard.

"He is such a showoff!" Dan muttered.

It didn't take long for the superspeed plane to reach Moscow. Michael's lab was a tall, dome-shaped stone tower attached to the main house. Kato expertly landed the plane in a grassy clearing nearby.

The doors to the lab slid open. Runo stepped inside first. Dan, Marucho, Alice, and Shun followed her. Drago, Tigrerra, and Preyas rolled on the stone floor next to them.

"Is anybody home?" she called out.

The lab was dark and empty. "There's no one here," Dan said.

"It kinda looks lived-in," Runo remarked.

"I must admit, Alice, I didn't expect it to be so clean," Marucho said. "I was expecting it to be much dustier, with cobwebs all over the place."

"That's because I come by every once in awhile and clean," Alice explained.

Dan looked around the large lab in awe. "And I thought tidying up my room was tough!"

"Well, if there are any clues to where my grandfather is, they would be here," Alice said.

"Okay, guys, let's split up and see what we can find!" Runo said eagerly.

Dan nodded. "Right! Let's do this!"

Drago, Tigrerra, and Preyas stayed by the front door.

"Tigrerra, do you feel it?" Drago asked.

"Yes, Drago, I do," she replied. She sounded concerned.

Preyas was bouncing up and down. "Yeah, since we got here, I've been feeling really jumpy. I can't seem to shake it! I just want to jump up and down! Up and down! Over and over!"

"You're always jumpy, Preyas," Drago pointed out.

"Whoa! Lighten up, Draggie!" Preyas shot back. He bounced with every word he said. "You're the one that brought up the weird feeling in this place!"

Preyas jumped again, and this time, he went flying up. He landed on a curved metal pipe. Then he slid down and landed on a button on a computer panel. A large screen on the back wall of the room flashed on.

"Oopsy!" Preyas said. An old man with white hair, a thin mustache, and a small goatee was talking on the screen.

"Yikes! What a face!" Preyas cried.

Alice gasped. "My grandfather!"

"This is Michael G.," the man said. "I am recording this from my research lab. Extraordinary things have been happening."

Julie was trying to watch from the video screen on Marucho's Baku-pod. "Hey, let me see what's going on!"

Marucho focused the Baku-pod on the screen as Michael continued his story.

"For the last few years I have been developing a Dimension Transporter System," he went on. "The system is designed to transport something from one place to another place in an instant. But one day while working in my laboratory something very unusual happened."

A video of the device appeared. The transporter looked like a large rectangular box with a screen on the front. Michael stood in front of the screen as it sizzled with energy, and then shattered into pieces. Inside, a whirling black vortex appeared. Michael screamed as he got pulled inside.

"There was a major accident," Michael explained. "Although I didn't know it at the time, I later learned that I had opened a gate to a different world. It was a place called Vestroia, and as unbelievable as it sounds, there were monsterlike creatures living there."

Dan nodded. He could believe it, all right. Michael had found the world of Bakugan!

"And there I was, face to face with the Dragonoid called Naga. He showed me a strange-looking card. Then he sent me flying back through the vortex," Michael remembered. "When I came to, I was back in the human world."

Now the video on the screen showed Michael examining a Bakugan card under a scanner.

"In our world, six months had passed by," Michael continued. "And that's not all. The accident with the transporter caused all of the protons of the field energy to collapse. As a result, these protons fell to Earth as card-shaped bodies. During the six months that I was gone, children used the cards to create the Bakugan game."

Dan and Shun exchanged glances. Together, they had created the rules of Bakugan.

"I was alarmed when I realized that these card-shaped energy bodies were absorbing the living creatures of Vestroia," Michael said. "It seems these creatures can only stay in the human world in the form of a ball. It is only on the battlefield that they can go back to their original forms."

Suddenly static filled the screen, and then the picture went blank.

"Darn! Come on! Finish the story!" Dan said, disappointed.

"Chill out," Runo told him. "At least now we know that Alice's grandfather went to Vestroia. So it's all true."

The screen flashed on again. Michael was back — but

he looked different. His skin was green and his hair was purple. He wore a black cape with a wide yellow collar.

"Huh? Grandfather?" Alice asked.

"I am Hal-G. Bow down before me!" he cackled. "Vestroia and the human world will be destroyed . . . by the power of the great Naga!"

# CHAPTER 6

## MINUS POWER

**H**al-G swirled his black cape and gave a sinister laugh. Then the screen went blank again.

"What happened to him?" Alice asked.

"It's the effects of minus power," Drago said.

"Minus power?" Dan asked.

Tigrerra spoke up, perched on Runo's shoulder. "When we arrived here, Drago, Preyas and I all felt the minus power in this place."

"Yeah, it makes me jumpy!" Preyas said, bouncing up and down on the control panel. "Look how jumpy I am! I can't stop jumping up and down! Up and down! Over and over! Somebody help me!"

"Whoa! That minus power really has an effect on you guys!" Runo observed.

Shun looked down at Skyress. The green Bakugan sat on his shoulder. "You feel it?"

"Yes, all Bakugan that are exposed to minus power find their inner darkness grows and they become ferocious," Skyress explained. "I suppose it's the same with humans as well."

"Over here!" Marucho cried.

He was fiddling with the controls, trying to rewind the video they had just seen. He focused on a figure hidden in the shadows behind Hal-G.

"I saw something on the video screen," Marucho said. "Wait. I'll zoom in."

The misty figure became a little bit clearer. It was a young man in a white suit, with wild yellow hair . . .

"Oh no!" Alice gasped. "That's . . ."

"Masquerade!" Dan cried.

"Hal-G and Masquerade?" Shun said thoughtfully. "So they've been working together."

"That figures," Marucho said.

"Those creeps," Runo muttered.

Alice's eyes filled with tears. "My grandfather! It can't be!"

Drago was grim. "Hal-G said he works under Naga. So Naga must control Masquerade as well."

Dan was silent. That would explain why Masquerade

kept sending brawlers to defeat them. He wanted to pave the way for Naga to destroy the world.

That was pretty serious. But it didn't scare Dan. He wasn't going to let a clown like Masquerade beat him.

*Bring it on, Masquerade!*

# CHAPTER 7

## THE TEAM FALLS APART

The next few weeks were a whirl of Bakugan brawls.

Komba and Billy challenged Shun and Julie to a battle. It was close, but Shun and Julie won in the end.

Chan battled Dan in a contest of Pyrus Bakugan against Pyrus Bakugan. Dan's Dragonoid helped lead him to victory.

Julio went up against Runo and Marucho. It looked like the Battle brawlers would lose — until Dan jumped in to help them out.

Masquerade's all-star team was having trouble defeating Dan and his friends. But the brawlers suffered one huge defeat when Klaus battled Marucho. Klaus sent Marucho's friend Preyas to the Doom Dimension.

Since that happened, Marucho was sad all the time. He stayed with the Battle brawlers, but all he could think about was his lost friend.

The brawlers were on a mission to bring Komba back to his home in Kenya. Komba had realized that battling for Masquerade wasn't a good idea. Dan, Marucho, Runo, Shun, Julie, and Alice flew to Kenya with Komba. Now they were about to get back on the plane and head home. But there was a surprise waiting for them.

Three figures in black hooded robes stood on the wings of the plane, waiting for them.

"I guess you found us," Dan said.

"But how?" Alice wondered.

The three brawlers threw off their black robes. Each one had a serious-looking black Bakugan shooter strapped to their right arm.

"It doesn't matter how we got here," Klaus said. "We came here for a battle, and that's what we intend to do."

"Right! How about we battle three on three?" Chan asked.

"Sure! Let's do it!" Dan said eagerly.

Marucho shook his fists. "I want my revenge!" he shouted. "Remember how they took Preyas away from me!"

Julio stepped forward and nodded at Runo. "I wanna battle you! And I'll make sure things don't turn out like the last time!"

"You're on, cue ball!" Runo replied.

Klaus, Chan, and Julio jumped off the plane and faced Dan, Runo, and Marucho. All six players held up a Gate Card.

"Field Open!"

The Bakugan field formed, and then Klaus, Chan, and Julio produced Doom Cards. The sinister cards sank into the field and disappeared.

"Gate Card Set!" the six players shouted as they tossed out their cards.

The six cards formed two rows, three cards long, on the field between the players.

"Is this a battle or a staring contest?" Dan taunted.

"Very well, allow me to go first!" Klaus said. "Bakugan brawl!"

Klaus shot out an Aquos Griffon with a power level of 330 Gs. Griffon had the body and head of a lion, wings of an eagle, and a long, reptilelike tail.

"Hey, are you ready for me?" Dan asked. He put a Bakugan ball into his shooter. But Marucho stepped in front of him.

"Let me take him on!" Marucho said.

"Are you sure, Marucho?" Dan asked.

"I know I can beat him," Marucho said confidently. He was ready for revenge!

But Runo wasn't paying attention to her teammates. She threw a Haos Mantris onto the same card as Griffon. Her Mantris had 340 Gs. It looked like a big white-and-gold bug with a long neck and bulging eyes.

Drago floated between the brawlers. "The three of you must work together or you will never win this!" he urged.

"Not now, Drago," Dan said impatiently.

Klaus made his next move. "Gate Card Open! Cheering Battle Activate!"

The card underneath Griffon and Mantris turned over to reveal its special instructions.

"Cheering battle?" Dan asked.

"That's right," Klaus said, grinning. "And that means I can add another Bakugan. It'll be a big surprise for all of you. Now, who was it that wanted to battle me?"

He turned, fixing his gaze on Marucho. "Oh yes, I remember. It was Marucho. Lucky you. You get to see my very special Bakugan!"

Klaus shot a blue Bakugan ball onto the field. "Preyas Stand!"

Marucho gasped. Preyas? He thought Preyas had been sent to the Doom Dimension.

"I don't believe it!" Drago cried.

Marucho was stunned. It looked like his Preyas — same sharklike face, same fins, same scaly skin.

"Preyas, is it really you?" His eyes filled with tears. "Oh, Preyas!"

"There's something different about him," Tigrerra warned.

She was right. Preyas was growling like a wild beast, jumping around with his tongue hanging out.

"Preyas, what's wrong with you?" Marucho asked.

"Sorry to let you down, but this won't be much of a reunion for you two," Klaus said. "You see, things have changed. Preyas is no longer with the Bakugan Battle Brawlers. He belongs to me!"

Preyas jumped onto Griffon's back. Griffon's power jumped to 370 Gs. The Bakugan leaped across the field, slamming into Mantris. The sky above the field opened up, revealed a black, swirling portal to the Doom Dimension. The portal pulled Mantris inside.

"Oh no!" Runo cried.

Preyas cackled with laughter. Then he and Griffon returned to their Bakugan balls. They bounced into Klaus's hand. He caught them and grinned at Marucho.

Dan was furious. "Hey you! What did you do to Preyas?"

"Preyas has been exposed to a lot of negative power," Drago explained. "That's what makes him act so savagely."

Dan, Runo, and Marucho were all shaken up by seeing Preyas in his new, evil form. For awhile, it took away from their focus on the brawl.

Julio made his move next. He shot out a Haos Fear Ripper. Marucho tossed an Aquos Stinglash onto the card with Fear Ripper. Then Julio used an Ability Card that called for both he and Marucho to put a new Bakugan into the battle. Julio chose Haos Centipoid, and Marucho chose Aquos Lumulus. Now Julio's Bakugan had a total of 680 Gs, and Marucho's had a total of 670 Gs.

"This isn't good," Runo said. "Marucho needs more power!"

"This never would have happened if he'd let me go first," Dan said.

"Dan! This is not the time to be complaining!" Drago scolded him.

Julio had one more move up his sleeve — a Rapid Haos Ability Card. It allowed one of his teammates to add a Bakugan to the battle. He chose Klaus — and of course, Klaus chose Preyas.

"Preyas! It's me! Your old friend Marucho!" Marucho called out.

Preyas didn't answer him. He snarled and then jumped up on top of one of the curved fangs coming out of Centipoid's mouth. Fear Ripper jumped on the other fang. Then Centipoid charged at Limulus and Stinglash.

*Bam!* Preyas jumped off, knocking down Limulus.

*Bam!* Fear Ripper jumped off, knocking down Stinglash.

*Whoosh!* Marucho's two Bakugan were sucked up into the Doom Dimension.

"Preyas, you don't have to be this way!" Marucho cried. "You're not a monster! Go back to the way you were!"

# CHAPTER 8

## RUNO'S PLAN

**C**han and Dan faced off next: Chan's Pyrus Garganoid against Dan's Pyrus Warius. Dan thought he had the round won, but Chan used a tricky Gate Card to bring Klaus into the battle. He used Preyas to send Warius to the Doom Dimension.

"You scammer!" Dan yelled.

"Don't let it get to you, Dan," Drago warned. "Don't give in to your anger! He knows that we'll get upset if he uses Preyas to attack."

"You gotta do something, Dan!" Runo said urgently.

"What should I do?" Dan asked. He was frustrated.

"You could get the old Preyas back," Runo suggested. "That would be a start."

"Huh? That's easy for you to say," Dan snapped. "Can't you think of something better than that?"

Drago floated between them. "What are you two doing? We're in the middle of a battle!"

Dan and Runo turned their backs to each other. Now Tigrerra floated up.

"If there ever was a time to work together, it would be now," she said. "We can't afford to fight with one another anymore."

Runo slowly turned around. "Uh, they're right."

Dan nodded. "Hey, sorry, Runo."

"No Dan, I'm sorry!" Runo said.

"Are you done?" Chan called from across the field. "Could you save the romantic quarrels for later?"

"Aw, zip it!" Runo shot back. "It's not like that at all. Bakugan Brawl!"

Runo sent a white-and-gold Bakugan ball zipping out of her shooter. "Ravenoid Stand!"

Haos Ravenoid stood on a Gate Card on the field. It looked like a majestic bird with feathers made of white and gold armor.

Julio sent out his Haos Tentaclear to battle Ravenoid.

"Time for a little light show!" he announced. "Ability Card Activate! Tentaclear Blinder!"

A bright, white light shone from Tentaclear's giant eyeball. Runo, Dan, and Marucho shielded their eyes from the white-hot brightness.

"I can't see a thing!" Runo cried out. "Did they get Ravenoid?"

"If we wait around to see, Preyas will get our other Bakugan," Marucho said.

"No he won't!" Dan said forcefully. "I know I can get him back if we win this battle."

Runo turned. "Go on! We've got no choice! Even Marucho said we have to take him out!"

Dan didn't understand her. "Yoo-hoo! You obviously didn't hear a word I said, did you? If I win this I can get Preyas back to his old self again!"

"That's what I mean!" Runo insisted. "Tigrerra once told me that when a Bakugan loses a battle, there's a huge impact on its body! Right, Tigrerra?"

"Yes, that's true," Tigrerra replied. "My lady, are you thinking . . ."

Runo nodded. "Yeah! If Preyas loses this battle, the shock to his head will put him back to normal."

"Preyas once battled so hard he forgot who he was," Drago remembered. "But when we walloped him on the head that brought him back to normal."

"Okay, but he's Klaus's Bakugan now," Dan reminded everyone. "If we do figure out a way to defeat him, won't he just go right back to Klaus again?"

"I already thought of that!" Runo said. "Just leave it to me."

"If you say so, Runo," Dan replied. "Klaus wants to mess with us so I know he'll bring Preyas out again. When he does, that's when I'll make my move!"

Tentaclear's bright light finally faded. Ravenoid was gone, banished to the Doom Dimension.

Chan made the next move. She threw out a Gate Card, and then shot a Pyrus Gargonoid with 340 Gs. Dan had Dragonoid stand on the Gate Card with Gargonoid. With 400 Gs, Dragonoid was poised to beat the Bakugan that looked like a stone gargoyle with wings.

Then Chan turned over the Gate Card.

"Triple battle!" she called out. "It's a Gate Card that can only be used when there are three Bakugan out on the battlefield. And the third one is right here."

Klaus chuckled. "Chan, once again you've set me up perfectly. You are too kind."

Klaus shot Preyas out onto the card with Gargonoid and Drago. He smiled confidently.

"This will be the end of Dan's Pyrus Dragonoid," he said. "Masquerade will be pleased to hear that."

"I got news for you, pal!" Dan shouted. "You walked right into my trap. Here we go! Ability Card Activate! Rapid Fire!"

Dan tossed a card onto the Gate Card. It transformed into a ring of flames between Dragonoid and Gargonoid and Preyas.

"That's Rapid Fire!" Dan explained. "It gives you the ability to let another of yours or a teammate's Bakugan join in the battle, if you have a Fire Attribute Bakugan on the field. And I've been saving that Ability Card for you, Klaus. Time to brawl!"

Runo shot a Bakugan from her shooter. "Go get 'em, Tigrerra!"

In her true form, Tigrerra was a massive beast with white fur, a powerful body, and sharp fangs and claws. She roared on the card next to Dragonoid.

For the first time in the battle, Klaus looked worried. "What? Our Bakugan have a total power level of only six hundred and sixty."

"*Calculating opponent's Bakugan power level . . . seven hundred forty Gs,*" Klaus's Baku-pod reported.

"No, they tricked me!" Klaus cried. "I should have seen it coming!"

"It's been a while, Preyas," Drago said calmly.

Preyas just giggled and snarled like an animal.

"You'll remember us soon enough," Tigrerra said. "As soon as we battle!"

Tigrerra leaped into the air.

*Bam!* She collided with Gargonoid.

Dragonoid flew across the card.

*Wham!* He slammed into Preyas, knocking him over.

Preyas and Gargonoid transformed into Bakugan balls and rolled off the field. They were both out of the battle now.

"We got him!" Marucho cheered.

"I'll take it from here," Runo said. "Sit tight, Marucho. Gate Card Set!"

Runo tossed a Gate Card onto the field. Then she shot Tigrerra onto the card.

"Ah, big deal," Julio scoffed. "Go Centipoid! Bakugan Brawl! Centipoid Stand!"

The big, buggy Bakugan faced Tigrerra. Runo wasn't worried.

"Ability Card Activate!" she said. "Pure Light!"

Julio was puzzled. "What is Pure Light?"

"You can use that card to restore any Bakugan that's been lost, no matter whose side it's been on," Chan told him.

A ray of yellow sparkling light shot from the card. It reached across the field and circled Preyas's Bakugan ball.

"Preyas, come back to us!" Runo cried.

Preyas's Bakugan ball floated through the air and landed in Runo's hand. She gave it to Marucho.

Preyas's ball popped open. He shook his head from side to side. "Huh? What? Where am I?" He sounded back to normal again.

Marucho's eyes filled with tears. "Oh, Preyas!"

"Whoa, hold on. I remember now!" Preyas said clearly. "I lost a battle and was held captive."

Marucho began to sob with joy and relief.

"Everything's okay now, Marucho," Runo said gently.

"Um, sorry to bother you, sonny," Preyas told Marucho. "But you'll have to save the crying for later. There's something we need to do right now. I believe we have a score to settle with those guys."

Marucho dried his tears. "You're right, Preyas!" he said. He fixed his gaze on Klaus, Chan, and Julio. "This is where the battle *really* begins!"

I'll start!" "Runo said.

Her Tigrerra and Julio's Centipoid still faced each other on a Gate Card. Centipoid had 350 Gs and Tigrerra had 340.

"Gate Card Open!" Runo shouted. "Energy Merge!"

Julio wasn't expecting that move. "What the —?"

"Energy Merge is a Gate Card that allows a Bakugan to siphon up to one hundred Gs from the Bakugan that was shot last," Runo explained.

*"Energy Merge in effect,"* her Baku-pod reported. Centipoid's Gs dropped to 250, and Tigrerra's jumped to 440.

"This time it's personal!" Tigrerra growled. She charged across the field, glowing with the extra power. Then she slammed into Centipoid, sending it flying back to Julio.

"No! Impossible!" Julio cried.

Dan cheered. "We did it!"

"Okay you guys, now it's my turn," Marucho said.

He shot out an Aquos Siege, a Bakugan that looked like a knight in blue armor. Siege had a power level of 350 Gs.

Chan countered with her Fortress. The four-headed, four-armed Bakugan stood on the card across from Siege, ready to battle. Siege's power level increased to 450 Gs. But the round wasn't over yet.

*"Fortress Power Boost of 50 Gs,"* Chan's Baku-pod announced.

Marucho watched in alarm as 50 Gs drained off of Siege and transferred to Fortress.

Fortress's head spun around until the angry, green-eyed face glared at Siege. "I am Fortress! Master of the Flame! My anger will burn anything in my path!"

Fortress gave a sinister laugh. "Now you will feel my raaaaaaaaaage!"

He aimed all four swords at Siege. A wave of flame shot from the swords and engulfed Siege. The Bakugan cried out as he was sucked into the Doom Dimension.

Chan grinned. "Wow! That was way easy!"

"Stuff it!" Dan called back angrily. "Bakugan Brawl! Griffon Stand!"

Dan shot his Pyrus Griffon onto the field. Klaus countered by throwing a Gate Card onto the field next to Griffon. Then he shot his Pyrus Sirenoid onto that card.

Klaus laughed. "Ha! This is going to be easy . . . for me," he crowed. "Ability Card Activate! Dive Mirage!"

Marucho frowned. "I've got a bad feeling about this, Dan."

Sirenoid dove into the Gate Card underneath her like it was a pool of water. Then a blue hand broke through the card underneath Griffon. It was Sirenoid! She grabbed Griffon's leg.

"Ah! Gate Card Open!" Dan shouted.

"Dan, no!" Marucho blurted out. "With Klaus's Dive Mirage activated, your Gate Card is rendered completely useless!"

On the field, Sirenoid spoke to Griffon in a musical, hypnotic voice. "Yes, that's it. Come to me . . ."

Sirenoid pulled Griffon underwater. The dark portal overhead opened up, and Griffon disappeared into the Doom Dimension.

"Unreal!" Dan cried. "Runo, it's up to you!"

"No problem!" Runo said. "Gate Card Set!"

She tossed out a Gate Card, then shot out a Bakugan ball. Tigrerra roared and stood on the card.

"Ha!" Julio smirked. "Time to put kitty back in the kennel. Gate Card Set!"

Julio put a card right next to Tigrerra's card. Then he shot his Haos Fear Ripper onto the card.

Preyas floated up next to Marucho. "When is it my turn to two-step?" he asked.

"How about right now?" Marucho asked. "Bakugan Brawl! Preyas Stand!"

He shot Preyas onto the card with Fear Ripper. Preyas was back to his old, silly self. He twirled a flowery umbrella in front of his face, giggling.

"Have no fear," he said in a girly voice. Then he lowered the umbrella. "Preyas is here!"

*"Preyas enters at three-forty Gs,"* Marucho's Baku-pod announced. Fear Ripper had 330 Gs.

"Let's get this party started!" Marucho called out. "Ability Card Activate! Blue Stealth!"

"Watch!" Preyas said. "Now you see me, now you don't!"

Preyas slowly became invisible.

*"Preyas power increase by fifty Gs,"* the Baku-Pod announced. *"Fear Ripper decrease by fifty Gs."*

"How do you like it so far?" Marucho asked.

"Ha!" Julio laughed. "That was totally lame! I can

trump that second-grade move with my eyes closed, kid. Gate Card Open!"

Invisible Preyas taunted Fear Ripper. "You can't see me! Na na na na na . . ."

Julio yelled out in frustration. "The card won't open!"

Marucho smiled. "I hate to break it to you, but my Gate Card leaves your Gate Card useless."

"Oh, Mr. Ripper! Peekaboo, I see you!" Preyas sang. "Hey, lunkhead, I'm over here!"

Then Preyas reached out with an invisible foot and kicked Fear Ripper right in the chest. The Bakugan fell and turned back into a Bakugan ball. Marucho had won the round!

"Yeah!" Marucho cheered.

"You brat!" Julio shot back.

Klaus, Chan, and Julio were losing their grip on the battle. Chan made the next move. She threw out a Gate Card and then put her Pyrus Manion on it. Manion looked like an ancient Egyptian sphinx, with the body of a lion and face of a human.

Dan tossed out a Gate Card, and then shot his Drago onto the card with Manion. Chan countered with an Ability Card that gave Manion an extra 100 Gs. Now Manion stood at 450 Gs to Drago's 400.

But Dan had a card up his sleeve, too. He used Boosted Dragon to give Drago an extra 100 Gs. Armed with the extra power, Drago shot a flaming ball of fire at Manion. Chan's Bakugan bounced off of the card, defeated.

The attack left Drago's body glowing with orange fire.

"It's happening again!" Drago cried out. "My body — wait. That's it! Maybe I'm beginning to evolve!"

"That Drago is one amped-up Bakugan," Klaus said admiringly. "I think it would make a perfect addition to my collection."

"Nobody touches my Drago except me, Klaus!" Dan said angrily.

Klaus put his hand behind his back and held up two fingers. Chan and Julio saw him.

"It's the sign!" Chan whispered. They knew just what Klaus was planning.

First, he threw out a new Gate Card. It landed right next to Tigrerra's card. Then he threw Aquos Griffon onto the card next to Tigrerra.

"Come on, are you going to battle or what?" Runo complained. "We don't have all day!"

Julio made the next move. He put a Gate Card on the other side of Tigrerra's card. Then he put Tentaclear on the new card.

"I'm confused," Marucho told Dan and Runo. "Why isn't Griffon or Tentaclear making a move? Let's see. They've got water and light out there . . ."

He looked at Chan. She always used Fire Element Bakugan. "That's it!" Marucho cried.

"Spill it!" Preyas urged. "What's the big revelation, chief?"

"Don't you see it?" Marucho asked. "With the combination of water, light, and fire, they're going to activate the Triple Node Attack!"

"You sure?" Dan asked.

"Not good!" Runo added.

"Say, I've got a fabulous idea," Preyas chimed in. "What do you say — we run?"

Dan, Runo, and Marucho groaned.

"The Triple Node Ability works like this," Marucho explained. "When three players in one battle throw down a combination of either fire, water, and light or wind, earth, and Darkon, the power levels of each of those Bakugan increases by two hundred Gs!"

"Yo, Flex! I'm ready to do some damage!" Preyas said in a tough-guy voice. "Now let's get this shindig started 'cause I'm ready to party, yo!"

Marucho loaded Preyas's Bakugan ball into his shooter. "Locked and loaded!" he said confidently.

Klaus grinned. "That's it," he whispered. "Step right into our little trap."

He launched Preyas onto the card with Aquos Griffon. Klaus laughed.

"He fell for it! Gate Card Open!" Klaus shouted. "Mine Ghost Activated."

*Bam!* As soon as Preyas stepped on the card, there was an explosion.

"Preyas, look out!" Marucho cried.

But it was too late. Both Griffon and Preyas disappeared in a cloud of smoke. The smoke spiraled up to the sky, and then vanished into the Doom Dimension!

# CHAPTER 10

## DRAGO'S ON FIRE

**K**laus's Mine Ghost Ability wiped out *both* Bakugan!" said a stunned Dan.

"It was a Trap Card!" Runo blurted out.

"No!" Tigrerra roared. "Not again, Preyas!"

Dan was confused. "I don't get it. Why would he send Preyas *and* his own Griffon to the Doom Dimension?"

"Don't you get it?" Julio asked. "The Triple Node was just a diversion for Klaus to use his Mine Ghost."

"And not to brag or anything, losers, but it looks like our little plan worked to perfection," Chan said smugly.

Klaus's smile was sinister. "This time your Preyas is stuck in the Doom Dimension forever," he said. "But I'm sure Griffon will keep him company."

"Not so fast, Quick Draw! This fight ain't over yet!"

Preyas's voice echoed across the field. An empty Gate Card began to swirl like water. Preyas rose up from the card.

"Ta-daaa!"

Chan, Klaus, and Julio looked shocked. Marucho smiled.

"It worked! My Dive Mirage saved Preyas," he said.

"What Dive Mirage move?" Dan asked.

"I'll explain," Marucho said. "When I sensed Klaus was going to use his Mine Ghost, I activated my Dive Mirage Ability. Preyas dove to the other card before Griffon was sent to the Doom Dimension."

"That was so cool!" Runo said. "Way to go."

"Hey, it was nothing," Marucho said modestly. "I'm just glad I didn't lose Preyas again!"

Klaus was angry. He had sacrificed his Bakugan for nothing! "So, you think you're pretty smart don't you?"

"Smarter than you'll be, Klaus Von Stupid!" Preyas taunted him.

Chan pointed at Preyas. "You're mine, Preyas. Bakugan Brawl!"

Chan threw Fortress onto the card with Julio's Tentaclear. Tigrerra was still on a card all by herself. Preyas was on a card by himself, too.

"Gate Card Open!" Chan cried. "Quartet Battle Activated!"

"I know that move," Marucho said. "It's one where all the Bakugan are forced to battle against each other."

Runo nodded. "Yeah, and it's up to them to choose who they want to battle against. Not to mention, we can throw in any new Bakugan!"

Dan quickly threw Drago onto the card. Klaus launched his Sirenoid into the battle.

"Oh no!" Runo said, worried. "It looks like it's Fortress, Tentaclear, and Sirenoid against your Drago, Dan!"

"Oh, snap!" Dan said. "That's three against one! That's not good."

His Baku-pod quickly calculated the power levels on the card. Drago had 500 Gs, but Tentaclear, Fortress, and Sirenoid had 1110 Gs combined.

"What do I do, guys?" Dan asked. He sounded nervous for the first time during the battle.

"Ya gotta put me in, coach!" Preyas pleaded.

"Yes, I too feel useless," said Tigrerra.

"Now that our Battle Ability is activated, you can use any of your useless Ability Cards that you like against it," Chan told them.

"I'm really not much of a team player, but this way, our win is guaranteed," Klaus said with confidence.

It looked like it was all a game of points. Klaus used an Ability Card to raise Siren's G power. Now it was 1210 Gs against Drago's 500.

Marucho used a card to give an extra 200 Gs to each of the Bakugan on their team. Bad guys, 1210, Drago, 700.

But Julio had an Ability Card, too. He boosted Tentaclear, and the numbers jumped to 1310 against Drago's 700 Gs. Things didn't look good for Drago.

"I have an idea, guys," Runo whispered to Dan and Marucho. "It's down to this card — Tigrerra's Cut In Slayer Ability. It's a risk, but we don't have a choice. Once I throw down a card, all of our Bakugan's power will go way up. But if one of our Bakugan is defeated, it can't go back into battle. In other words, we're history!"

"If it is our only hope, then it is a risk we must take," Drago said firmly.

Tigrerra and Preyas agreed. Runo threw the card onto the field.

"Ability Card Activate! Cut In Slayer!"

Tigrerra and Preyas faded from their cards and appeared next to Drago.

"This is for all Bakugan!" she said. She returned to her ball, but stayed on the card.

"Preyas present and ready for action!" Preyas cried. He turned into a ball, too.

"With you two at my side, we cannot fail!" Drago said gratefully.

Tigrerra and Preyas couldn't battle, but they could give their power to Drago. Together, their power now reached 1780 Gs!

But there was more to come. The field split open under Drago's feet. Flames leaped up through the cracks.

*"Power surge detected,"* Dan's Baku-pod reported. Drago's Gs began to rise, point by point.

The flames engulfed him, forming a huge ball that floated in the air. Then the flames hardened like lava, forming a strange cocoon around Drago.

Dan was amazed. "Man, I've never seen anything like this before," he said. "Drago! Drago!"

"I've got to put a stop to this," Chan said. "Ability Card Activate! Water and light!"

Chan's card spiked the power levels of all of the Bakugan on her team. Now they had an incredible 1910 Gs. Unless he got another big power boost, Drago would lose the battle.

*Pow! Pow! Pow!*

Drago burst through the lava cocoon. He looked bigger, stronger, and more powerful than before.

"Drago! You've evolved!" Dan cried out.

Drago gave a ferocious roar. "So this is what my new body feels like!" he cried. "Pyrus Delta Dragonoid!"

Drago's power jumped to 1830 Gs.

"Oh, wow, that is totally off the charts!" Julio said.

Chan was annoyed. "Okay, did we win the battle or not?"

Klaus grinned. "Oh yeah! Cause we still have more Gs than Drago. But was there ever any doubt?"

They all laughed, thinking they had won the battle. But since Drago was in a new form, Dan was allowed to use another Ability Card.

"Ability Card Activate! Attack!"

Klaus, Chan, and Julio watched in shock as Drago's points climbed up to 2030 Gs.

"We're toast," Klaus said.

A blazing fireball formed in Drago's mouth. He hurled a barrage of fireballs at Tentaclear, Sirenoid, and Fortress. They cried out as Drago blasted them off the field.

The Bakugan field vanished around them. The battle was over.

Dan, Runo, and Marucho had won!

# CHAPTER 11

## DAN'S CHALLENGE

The battle with Dan, Runo, and Marucho set Klaus, Julio, and Chan free from Masquerade's spell. They tossed away the Doom Cards and Bakugan shooters Masquerade had given them. Then they all went back home.

Dan, Runo, and Marucho went back home, too. Julie, Shun, and Alice stuck with them. A few days later they were all in Runo's restaurant, waiting for Masquerade's next move. Runo and Alice were waiting tables. Dan and the others sat at one of the restaurant's round tables.

Then they got a surprise visit from Joe, the webmaster of the Bakugan website. Joe was a tall boy with shaggy brown hair and gray-blue eyes. He had some bad news for the brawlers.

"Masquerade — he took down Chan," Joe said.

Everyone gasped. Chan's Fortress had been sent to the Doom Dimension!

"You're kidding!" Dan cried.

Joe nodded. "And it's not only Chan. I got some serious information that Julio was hit by him as well."

"Julio too?" Runo asked.

"I guess that means . . . he got to Billy," Julie said sadly, thinking of her childhood friend.

"Most likely," Joe said. "He probably got his other sidekicks, too."

The brawlers thought about this. Julio, Komba — they must have lost their Bakugan forever, too.

Dan slammed his fist down on the table. "Rats!" he yelled. "It's got to be revenge! He's getting revenge on all of them!"

Joe shook his head. "No, Dan. I think there's more to all of this than simple revenge."

"He's probably trying to increase Hydranoid's power level, in order to make him evolve," Drago said.

"Makes sense," Tigrerra agreed. "Fortress and Sirenoid were very powerful Bakugan."

Marucho looked worried. "But then that could mean . . ."

"That could mean that Hydranoid has already evolved!" Julie finished for him.

The thought of Hydranoid evolving was a scary one. Masquerade's Darkus Hydranoid was already very powerful. The vicious Bakugan was cruel and merciless in battle. If it evolved, it would be even more dangerous.

Dan jumped up on the table. "I say bring it on!" he shouted, pounding his fist in the air. "'Cause Drago's already evolved. So quit hanging out in the shadows like the chicken I know you are, Masquerade!"

That night, Dan had trouble sleeping. He was anxious to battle Masquerade, to end things once and for all. What was Masquerade waiting for?

Then a strange feeling came over Dan. He opened his eyes as a shadow crossed over his pillow. He sat up.

Masquerade was floating over his bed!

Dan quickly jumped out of bed. "It's Masquerade. What are you doing here?"

Masquerade vanished like a ghost. Then Dan heard his voice behind him.

"You were the one who asked me to come out of the shadows."

Dan spun around, pointing. "Oh yeah, and I called you a chicken, too! I want to brawl right here and now!"

Masquerade vanished again.

"Where'd he go?" Dan growled.

Then he heard Masquerade's laugh behind him again. The masked brawler was hanging upside down from the ceiling like a bat!

"Easy, tough guy. I've already decided the time and place," Masquerade said. He produced a card in his right hand. "And then we'll see who's . . . chicken!"

Masquerade threw the card at Dan.

Everything went black. Dan found himself in bed again. He sat up.

"I'm no chicken!" he cried.

He took a deep breath. "Guess it was a dream."

Then he noticed something on the floor — Masquerade's invitation.

"It was real!" Dan realized. His brown eyes shone with determination. "Masquerade, I've had enough! I'm gonna take you down for everything you've done!"

# CHAPTER 12

## THE SHOWDOWN BEGINS

**P**ink clouds streaked the sky at sunset the next night. Dan walked down a deserted street in the town's warehouse district. With each step he took, he thought of Drago. His Bakugan had battled bravely beside him time after time. He wasn't going to let Drago down.

Runo was waiting for Dan in front of one of the buildings. She joined Dan, walked in step beside him. Next came Julie and Marucho.

Shun jumped off a roof, landing next to Runo. The five Battle brawlers marched to meet Masquerade.

The masked brawler was waiting for them at the end of the road.

Dan and his friends stopped. Dan pointed.

"Okay! Let's do this now!" he challenged.

Masquerade held up a Gate Card. "Go ahead and try."

The five Battle brawlers each held up a card.

"Field Open!" everyone shouted at once.

Purple and blue light swirled around them as the Bakugan field formed. Masquerade held up the sinister Doom Card.

"Doom Card Set!"

He dropped the card, and it sank into the field. Then Dan and Masquerade each set out a Gate Card onto the field.

Masquerade made the next move.

"Gate Card Set," he said, as he added a third card to the mix.

Then he loaded his black Bakugan shooter with a ball.

"Bakugan Brawl!" he cried. "Darkus Wormquake Stand!"

In its true form, Darkus Wormquake was a terrifying sight. The giant worm had a gaping mouth full of sharp teeth. Wormquake had 380 Gs.

"My turn!" Dan countered. "Bakugan Brawl! Pyrus Griffon Stand!"

Dan tossed his lionlike Bakugan onto the card with Wormquake. At 390 Gs, Griffon was more powerful than Wormquake. But Masquerade turned over the Gate Card to reveal Energy Merge. One hundred Gs were transferred from Griffon to Wormquake. Now Wormquake had 480 Gs, and Griffon only had 290.

"You think that'll stop me?" Dan asked. "Ability Card Activate! Fire Tornado!"

Griffon's eyes glowed red as the power of the card took hold. A swirling ring of flame whipped around the card. Wormquake quickly began to lose energy.

*"One hundred Gs transferred back to Pyrus Griffon,"* Dan's Baku-pod reported.

The tornado of flame slammed into Wormquake, sending the Bakugan flying off the field.

"So the first win goes to Dan," Runo remarked.

"I win!" Dan cried.

"That time," Masquerade said. "Bakugan Brawl! Darkus Laserman Stand!"

The black robot-like Bakugan towered over the field. Laserman had a strong metal body and a powerful cannon on top of each shoulder.

*"Power level, three-seven-zero Gs,"* said the Baku-pod.

"Three seventy? Think I'll go with Griffon again," Dan said. He shot Griffon onto the card with Laserman.

Griffon pounced, ready to take down Laserman.

"All right, Gate Card open," Masquerade said. "Joker's Wild."

A purple mist floated up from the center of the card. It trapped Griffon. Dan watched in horror as the mist carried Griffon into the Doom Dimension!

"Oh no, Griffon!" Dan cried. He turned to Masquerade, angry. "What was that? They hadn't even brawled yet!"

"The Joker's Wild Card," Masquerade said, sounding pleased with himself. "With it, the Darkus Bakugan wins unconditionally."

"I've never heard of that card before," Julie remarked.

"Things are getting serious," Marucho told her. "Both Dan and Masquerade only have two Bakugan left now."

"You're right, Marucho, things really are getting serious," Shun said darkly. "More serious than you could ever imagine."

Masquerade threw down a Gate Card. Then he shot Darkus Laserman onto the card.

"What? He's using Darkus Laserman again?" Dan asked.

"Just be careful, Dan," Shun warned. "Masquerade has something up his sleeve."

"Ha!" Dan laughed. "When I'm done he's gonna wish he had never got dressed."

Dan threw out a Gate Card. Then he shot a Bakugan ball onto the card with Laserman.

"Pyrus Saurus Stand!"

A Bakugan that looked like a tough red dinosaur appeared. He had a horn on his nose and two on top of his face. His skin looked like plated armor.

"*Saurus, ten G advantage*," reported the Baku-pod. Saurus had 380 Gs compared to Laserman's 370.

"Okay, Pyrus Saurus! Let's show this chump who rules this playground!" Dan shouted.

Saurus charged across the card. "Gate Card Open," Masquerade said calmly.

*Pow!* Saurus punched Laserman. The robotic Bakugan went flying off the field.

"He did it!" Dan cheered.

But then something strange happened. Saurus began to sink into the Gate Card! Only the top half of his body was sticking out above the card.

"Oh no! I've heard of this!" Marucho cried out. "It's called Quicksand Freeze!"

Masquerade laughed. "It's showtime! And now for the main attraction." He opened up his palm, and a black and purple Bakugan ball floated up. A glowing purple mist swirled around the ball.

"Dual Hydranoid!"

# CHAPTER 13

## DAN'S LAST STAND

Runo gasped. "So it's true, then."

Masquerade loaded his Bakugan shooter.

"Bakugan Brawl! Dual Hydranoid Stand!"

The Bakugan brawlers watched openmouthed as the massive Bakugan took shape in front of them. Dual Hydranoid was a dragonlike beast with two heads and two long necks. The tough skin on its body was a sleek, purple-black color and looked almost like metal. Its eyes glowed red, and each mouth was filled with knifelike red teeth. Sharp spikes cascaded down its back, and its hand ended in sharp claws. It looked like something straight out of a nightmare.

"This is Hydranoid evolved!" Dan cried.

*"Power level four-seven-zero Gs,"* announced the Baku-pod.

Dual Hydranoid roared, and a hot, foul wind assaulted Dan and his friends.

"What the heck was that?" Preyas wondered.

"Well, the stage is now set," Masquerade said. "But all of the actors have yet to arrive."

"What?" Dan asked.

Masquerade grinned at Dan. "Come, my friend. It's your turn."

Drago floated up to Dan.

"It looks like it's your turn, old buddy," Dan said.

"I am ready," Drago replied.

Dan grabbed Drago and loaded him into his Bakugan shooter.

"This is it. Good luck," Dan told his friend. He shot Drago onto the Gate Card with Dual Hydranoid. "Bakugan Brawl! Drago Stand!"

Drago burst onto the field in a wall of burning flame.

"*Drago at four-five-zero Gs,*" Dan's Baku-pod reported.

"Well, it looks like we have a full cast," Masquerade said.

Dual Hydranoid glared at Drago. "It looks like two heads are better than one!" said one of its heads.

"Plus three is a crowd," growled the other.

"Well, one works for me," Drago retorted. "So that doesn't leave much room for you."

Dan opened the Gate Card underneath them. The face of the card burned with flame, giving Drago an extra power boost.

"Brawl!" Dan commanded.

The two giants lunged at each other. Dual Hydranoid smacked Drago with its long, spiked tail. Drago lashed out, jabbing Dual Hydranoid with the sharp point on the end of his wing. Dual Hydranoid chomped onto Drago's shoulder. Drago roared and reared back, pounding Dual Hydranoid with a powerful punch. The two Bakugan were evenly matched.

"How do you like the show so far?" Masquerade asked. He held up a card. "I think perhaps it's time for Dual Hydranoid to bring the house down. Ability Card Activate! Dual Gazer."

A glowing white ball formed in each of Dual Hydranoid's mouths. One ball shot across the field, zapping Pyrus Saurus on the card behind them.

"But — how?" Drago wondered.

The beast's other head was fixed on Drago, ready to destroy him with a ball of light.

"Drago, watch out!" Dan shouted.

*"Dual Hydranoid increase five-zero Gs,"* said the Baku-pod.

Now Dual Hydranoid had 530 Gs to Drago's 520. Dan knew he had to act fast.

"Ability Card Activate! Wall Burst!"

There was a small explosion on the field. A cloud of white smoke shrouded the two Bakugan.

"Did it work?" Dan wondered.

*"Dual Hydranoid decrease by one hundred Gs."*

Dual Hydranoid was left with only one head — and 430 Gs.

"Yeah!" Dan cheered.

"Well, well, the plot thickens," Masquerade said. He laughed. "Congratulations. You've succeeded in making me very angry."

Masquerade threw a card in the air. The card shattered — and Dual Hydranoid's head grew back!

"No way!" Dan cried.

"Unbelievable," Drago said. The battle wasn't over yet, but the round was over. The Bakugan returned to Dan and Masquerade.

"Now it's time for the final curtain," Masquerade said. He loaded Dual Hydranoid into his shooter. "And unfortunately for you there will be no encores. Playtime's over."

He launched his Bakugan into the field. Dan gazed down at Drago in his palm.

"I've gotta put you back in, Drago," Dan said. "Let's finish this once and for all."

"I'm ready, Dan," Drago replied. "Ready to do everything I can to take down Dual Hydranoid."

He floated in front of Dan's face. "Listen, Dan. We can only do this together."

Dan nodded. "Yeah!"

He shot Drago onto the card with Dual Hydranoid.

"Okay, this is it, Masquerade," Dan said. His brown eyes blazed with energy. He was not going to lose! "Gate Card Open! Character Card Activate!"

The two Bakugan were standing on Drago's character card. Drago's Gs doubled to a whopping 900 points.

Masquerade held up a card. "Ability Card Activate. Gazer Exedra!"

That card boosted Dual Hydranoid's power to 580 Gs — but that still wasn't enough to beat Drago.

"Check this out," Dan said, holding up a card. "Delta Dragonoid!"

Drago roared as his power jumped 400 points to 1300 Gs.

"There is no way you can beat us!" Dan said.

"On the contrary," Masquerade replied calmly. "We can beat you, and we will. Fusion Ability Card Activate! Destruction Impact!"

"Delta Hydranoid power increase one hundred Gs."

Drago got ready to launch a fireball at his opponent. "Delta Dragonoid!" he cried.

Drago flew up into the air and blasted his opponent with a blazing wall of fire.

"Woo-hoo!" shouted Julie.

"Way to go!" Marucho cheered.

"Good job, you two," said Runo.

"Yes!" Shun said.

"Told ya!" Dan called out. "There's no way that — what?"

The smoke cleared — and Delta Hydranoid was still standing!

"So tell me, was that your best shot?" the Bakugan asked.

"I don't get it," Dan said. "There's no way he could have survived that."

He looked at his Baku-pod, hoping for some explanation.

*"Drago power level six-five-zero Gs."*

"But why?" Dan asked. "Why did Drago's power level go down?"

"Destruction Impact doesn't just boost Hydranoid's power level — it also cancels out your Gate Card," Masquerade explained. His evil laugh echoed across the field.

"It can't be," Dan said, his heart sinking. "It just can't be. It's not possible."

"Looks like this show is over — for you at least," Dual Hydranoid growled.

Masquerade motioned to his Bakugan. "And now, Dual Hydranoid, time to take a bow."

With a hideous cry, Dual Hydranoid reared back both of its heads. Then it began to shoot out a barrage of glowing laser blasts.

*Bam! Bam! Bam!* The glowing purple balls of energy pounded Drago.

"No, please, don't do this to him!" Dan pleaded.

"This can't be!" Marucho cried.

"I can't watch!" Preyas added.

Bam! Another blast slammed into Drago. He started to fall backward.

"Dan, farewell, my friend."

Masquerade sneered. "Away with you."

The Doom Dimension portal opened up. Drago rose up into the air. Dan chased after him.

"No! I won't let you go like this!" Dan cried.

"Wait, Dan!" Shun called out. He took off after Dan. But Dan was too fast. "I'll never leave you!"

He jumped up into the air. The pull of the Doom Dimension lifted him up.

"Wait for me!" Dan yelled.

Then the portal closed.

Dan and Drago were both trapped inside the Doom Dimension!

**S**hun, Julie, Runo, and Marucho were stunned.

"What happened?" Runo asked, her blue eyes wide.

"That was foolish," Masquerade said.

The Bakugan field disappeared around them. The sun shone in the pink sky once more.

Runo started to cry. "Dan? Where are you, Dan?"

Then she got angry. She stepped toward Masquerade. "What have you done to him? Tell me!"

"I have done nothing to him. He chose his own fate," Masquerade replied. "The Doom Dimension is the after-life for Bakugan. There is no return for Bakugan — or humans."

Runo started to cry again. Shun was furious. "You did this!" he told Masquerade. He charged after the masked brawler — but Masquerade vanished.

Marucho fell to his knees. Julie was sobbing now, too. "Oh, Dan! Why did you have to go and do that?"

Hot tears fell from Marucho's eyes. "Oh no, no, no!"

Tigrerra floated onto Runo's shoulder. "Oh, Runo," she said sadly.

Runo gazed up at the sky.

"Daaaaaaaaaaaan!"

Her heart felt like breaking.

Would they ever see Dan again?

# HOW DO YOU ROLL?™

ROLL WITH THE SKILL OF A MASTER BRAWLER AND ACHIEVE TRUE BATTLE GLORY!
GRAB YOUR FAVORITE BAKUGAN™ AND UNLEASH YOUR INNER WARRIOR AS YOU
WATCH YOUR BAKUGAN™ TRANSFORM INTO AWESOME, POWERFUL BEASTS!
THE TIME FOR BATTLE IS NOW, ONLY YOU CAN DECIDE THE FATE OF THE GALAXY!

VISIT **BAKUGAN.COM** TO LEARN MORE ABOUT BAKUGAN™ BATTLE BRAWLERS.™

TM SPIN MASTER LTD AND © 2008 SPIN MASTER LTD/SEGA TOYS.